D1063789

STONE ARCH BOOKS
a capstone imprint

STONE ARCH BOOKS™

Published in 2013
A Capstone Imprint
1710 Roe Crest Drive
North Mankato, MN 56003
www.capstonepub.com

Originally published by DC Comics in the U.S. in single magazine form as Batman Adventures #5.

DC Comics
1700 Broadway, New York, NY 10019
A Warner Bros. Entertainment Company

Printed in China by Nordica.
0413/CA21300442
032013 007226NORDF13

Cataloging-in-Publication Data is available at the Library of Congress website:
ISBN: 978-1-4342-6033-8 (library binding)

Summary: Private detective Harvey Bullock is chained to a suitcase that everyone wants, including a marksman named Deadshot! Can Batman keep him off-target? Plus, in the backup story, learn how Bullock lost his badge.

STONE ARCH BOOKS

Ashley C. Andersen Zantop *Publisher*
Michael Dahl *Editorial Director*
Donald Lemke & Sean Tulien *Editors*
Heather Kindseth *Creative Director*
Bob Lentz & Alison Thiele *Designers*
Kathy McColley *Production Specialist*

DC COMICS

Joan Hilty *Original U.S. Editor*
Harvey Richards *U.S. Assistant Editor*
Kelsey Shannon *Cover Artist*

TARGET: DEADSHOT!

Dan Slott .... writer
Ty Templeton .... penciller
Terry Beatty .... inker
Lee Loughridge .... colorist
Phil Felix .... letterer

Batman created by
Bob Kane

GOTHAM CITY, ONE YEAR AGO.
THIS IS RICKY SQUIB, PRIVATE EYE.
NOT THE KIND YOU SEE ON TV, WITH THE FAST CARS AND THEIR OWN THEME MUSIC.
GOTHAM ARMS HOTEL
GOTHAM ARM
C'MON, YOU DIRTY BIRD...
...GIMME SOMETHING I CAN USE!
NO--RICKY'S THE KIND THAT DIGS THROUGH YOUR TRASH AND LOOKS THROUGH YOUR BEDROOM WINDOW.
HILL FOR MAYOR
KLIK KLIK!
OH YEAH! THAT'S IT! THESE ARE KEEPERS!
NOT THE MOST GLAMOROUS JOB. BUT HE ALWAYS FELT THAT IF HE KEPT AT IT, THAT ONE DAY HE'D FINALLY GET HIS SHOT--
COBBLEPOT FOR MAY
KLIK KLIK!
--HIS MILLION-DOLLAR SHOT!
13A
14

AND FOR OUR FINAL ORDER OF BUSINESS, GENTLEMEN--
--A HIGH-PRICED HIT.
GOTHAM CITY, TONIGHT.
AT THE SECRET HEADQUARTERS OF BLACK MASK AND HIS FALSE FACE SOCIETY.
A LOW-END GUMSHOE BY THE NAME OF RICKY SQUIB HAS BEEN PUTTING THE SQUEEZE ON MY NEW "CLIENT."
HE'S TO BE ELIMINATED.
ALONG WITH THIS VALISE HE'S BEEN CARRYING...
ITS CONTENTS...
KLIK
...AND ANYONE WHO'S COME INTO CONTACT WITH IT.
DEADSHOT?
SHOULDN'T TAKE LONG.
SOMEONE ORDER A PIZZA. I'LL BE RIGHT BACK.
DAN SLOTT · TY TEMPLETON · TERRY BEATTY · LEE LOUGHRIDGE · PHIL FELIX · H. RICHARDS · JOAN HILTY
WRITER PENCILLER INKER COLORIST LETTERER ASSISTANT ED. EDITOR
SHOT TO THE HEART
UNGH--
BATMAN CREATED BY BOB KANE

MESSAGE:
MAYOR COBBLEPOT CARES

S-SURE! ANYTHING YOU WANNA KNOW! ANY SUBJECT UNDER THE SUN--
THE PENGUIN.
I GOT NOTHING ON HIM, BATS! HONEST! HOW ABOUT BLACK MASK? I GOT TONS OF DISH ON THAT GUY!
A PETTY CROOK. DON'T WASTE MY TIME, EEL.
YOU'RE KIDDING, RIGHT? THE MASK IS ANGLING TO BE THE NEXT BIG CRIME BOSS FOR ALL A' GOTHAM!
YOU'D KNOW THAT IF YOU WEREN'T SO BUSY WITH YOUR VENDETTA AGAINST THE MAYOR!

YOU'D BE SO NICE, YOU'D BE PARADISE, TO COME HOME TO AND LOVE.
HOW ODD. A PIECE SEEMS TO BE MISSING FROM MRS. WAYNE'S JEWELRY COLLECTION.
BUT WHICH ONE?
AH YES, NOW I REMEMBER...
YOU REALLY LIKE THAT, DON'T YOU, BRUCE?
IT'S PRETTY, MOMMA.
WELL, WHY DON'T I SAVE IT FOR YOU? AND ONE DAY, YOU CAN GIVE IT TO THE WOMAN YOU LOVE.
IS SHE HERE YET, ALFRED? I'M NOT LATE, AM I?
NO, MASTER BRUCE, YOU'RE--
AH! THE MISSING PIECE.
SO, I TAKE IT YOUR RELATIONSHIP WITH MS. MADISON IS... PROGRESSING NICELY.
GIVING HER A PIECE OF YOUR MOTHER'S JEWELRY AND ALL.
IT'S JUST A TOKEN, REALLY. AFTER ALL, I HAVE BEEN SEEING JULIE FOR SIX MONTHS.
AND FOR ME THAT'S... WELL...

A RECORD, SIR?
YES, ALFRED.

FIRST THERE WAS ZATANNA.
WHO BECAME THAT MASKED KILLER PHANTASM, JUST AS MS. SELINA KYLE TURNED OUT TO BE CAT-WOMAN.
AND LADY TALIA, DAUGHTER OF THE FIENDISH RA'S AL GHUL. ALL WRONG FOR YOU, SIR.
THOUGH I WAS FOND OF MS. LANE...
THE MAGIC WAS THERE WITH ZANNA. BUT WE WERE FOREVER PULLING DIS-APPEARING ACTS ON EACH OTHER.
THEN THERE WAS ANDREA. ANDREA BEAUMONT...
LOIS? I DON'T THINK SO, ALFRED. WE ALL KNOW WHERE HER HEART REALLY LIES.
AH, YES. AND LEST WE NOT FORGET--
--THAT TIME POISON IVY TRICKED YOU INTO MARRYING A PLANT CREATURE.
MASTER BRUCE? OH, DEAR...
DING DONG!
MERCIFUL HEAVENS. SAVED BY THE BELL.
THE DOOR, PLEASE, ALFRED.

YOU'D BE SO NICE TO COME HOME TO
ALF SURE KNOWS HOW TO PLAN AN EVENING, DOESN'T HE?
I BET HE EVEN TAUGHT YOU THIS ADORABLE TWO-STEP.
YES. BUT THE DIP IS ALL MINE.
AND YOU DO IT SO WELL.
THANK YOU.
JULIE, THERE'S SOMETHING IMPORTANT I WANT TO TALK TO YOU ABOUT.
I WANT YOU TO HAVE THIS. IT USED TO BELONG TO MY MOTHER.
OH, THANK GOD! I THOUGHT IT WAS GOING TO BE ABOUT THE PENGUIN.

THE PENGUIN? WHY ON EARTH WOULD I WANT TO TALK ABOUT THE PENGUIN?
BRUCE, DARLING. THAT'S ALL YOU EVER WANT TO TALK ABOUT. I SWEAR, YOU'RE LIKE A DOG WITH A BONE.
BEEP BEEP

MUST BE WORK.
KLIK!
SHOULDN'T TAKE LONG.

I HAVE TO TAKE THIS.
RED PHONE

BRUCE WAYNE, DON'T YOU DARE!
I KNOW YOUR WORK IS IMPORTANT TO YOU, BUT NOT TONIGHT!

NOT RIGHT NOW!

I'M SORRY, JULIE. PERHAPS SOME OTHER NIGHT--
PERHAPS SOME OTHER LIFE!
GOOD-BYE, BRUCE.

THIS HAD BETTER BE AN EMERGENCY, BULLOCK!

BLAM!
BANG!
KPOW!
EMERGENCY?! OH, I GOT YOUR EMERGENCY, BATS!
KEESHH!
SOME YAHOO'S TURNIN' MY CAR INTO A SPAGHETTI STRAINER!

BRAK! KCHOW!
SCREECH!
WHAT HAVE YOU DONE NOW, HARVEY?
OH, NOT MUCH. JUST THE ONE THING YOU'VE BEEN PAYIN' ME TO DO...
...GET DIRT ON THE PENGUIN!
WAM!
PKOW!
KBAM!
I'M ALREADY ON MY WAY. WHATEVER YOU DO, KEEP THIS LINE OPEN--
--I'M HOMING IN ON YOUR SIGNAL.
HEH. BAD MOVE, MEAT. YOU JUST BOXED YOURSELF IN.
WON'T TAKE ME LONG TO FIND YOU AND THAT OLD PIECE A' JUNK YOU'RE DRIVIN'...
AW CRUD.
ON SECOND THOUGHT, THIS MIGHT TAKE A WHILE.
APARO'S
AUTO SCRAP YARD
"I AM SO OUT OF HERE, ALF!"

MS. MADISON, WAIT! SURELY THERE MUST BE SOME WAY FOR MASTER BRUCE TO MAKE AMENDS?
IF THERE IS, HE BETTER DO IT BEFORE THE NEXT FLIGHT TO STAR CITY!
AS FAR AS I'M CONCERNED, I'VE HAD ENOUGH OF THIS TOWN--
--AND ENOUGH OF "MASTER BRUCE"!
OH DEAR.
BRUCE! IF YOU HURRY YOU CAN STILL...
SIGH
IT APPEARS, ONCE AGAIN, THAT I MUST PICK UP AFTER YOU.
REGRETFULLY, THERE ARE SOME MESSES YOU WILL HAVE TO CLEAN UP FOR YOURSELF...
"...PROVIDING THERE'S STILL TIME."
HANG TIGHT, BULLOCK. I'M ALMOST THERE.
VROOOOOM!
NOW TELL ME, WHAT EXACTLY DO YOU HAVE ON PENGUIN?

WISH I KNEW, BATS. THE STUFF'S IN A LOCK-BOX. BUT WHATEVER IT IS...
IT'S WORTH MORE THAN MY LIFE... AND RICKY'S.
RICKY?
RICKY SQUIB, TWO-BIT SHAMUS AND ALL-AROUND BUM. WE GO WAY BACK. IN FACT, WHEN THE PENGUIN HAD ME THROWN OFF THE FORCE, RICKY TOOK ME IN. MADE ME HIS PARTNER.
AND TONIGHT, HE WAS CUTTIN' ME IN FOR PART OF HIS "BIG SCORE." ALL I HAD TO DO WAS WATCH HIS BACK.
SEEMS HE WAS BLACKMAILING SOMEBODY WITH A BUNCH OF INCRIMINATIN' PHOTOS. NORMALLY, I'D HAVE NUTHIN' TO DO WITH SOMETHING THAT SLEAZY...
BUT WHEN HE TOLD ME THE PICS CAME FROM HIS "COBBLEPOT FILE," THAT GOT MY UNDIVIDED ATTENTION!
PIZZA
WELL, THAT AND THE .45 CALIBER WAKE-UP CALL.
BLAM!
I'D MOURN FOR THE POOR SAP LATER.
THE IMPORTANT THING WAS TO GET THE GOODS, STAY ALIVE, AND GET 'EM TO YOU!
GOOD WORK, HARVEY. NOW GET MOVING. YOU CAN'T STAY THERE.
YEAH? TELL ME SOMETHIN' I DON'T KNOW.
I MEAN NOW, BULLOCK. AT LEAST TWO FEET TO YOUR RIGHT.

JEEZALOO!
KASSH!
BULLOCK!
YOU CRAZY, BATS?! YOU WUZ THIS CLOSE TO MY--
EXPLOSIVE ROUNDS! LOCK!
CH-CHOK!
FIRE!
FWEEEEE
GET DOWN!

KATHOOOM!
WHAT THE HECK WAS THAT?!
BETTER CALL IT IN!

REMEMBER ME, DARK KNIGHT?
LAST TIME, YOU NEEDED A WHOLE TEAM OF SUPERHEROES TO BEAT ME!
THEY WERE JUST IN MY WAY.
ALL I NEED TO TAKE YOU DOWN --
--IS ONE CLEAR SHOT.
FUNNY...
...I WAS THINKING THE EXACT SAME THING ABOUT YOU.
BANG!
HEY!
KRAK

WHOA!
FWIP!
HA! THAT THE BEST YOU GOT?

KLIK!
YOU MISSED ME BY A MI--

KUNCH!
AHH!

I NEVER MISS.
KRAK!
HEH. THAT'S ONE WAY TO GET THE DROP ON 'EM!
WEEOOO!
HEADS UP, BUL-LOCK. COMPANY.

WEEEOOoooo!
WELL, IF IT AIN'T MY OLD "PARTNER," CAPTAIN MONTOYA.
PARDON ME FOR NOT SALUTIN', RENEE. BUT MY HANDS ARE KINDA FULL AT THE MOMENT.
HARVEY? WHAT'S GOING ON? WHAT ARE YOU DOING HERE?
NOT MUCH! JUST GATHERIN' EVI-DENCE THAT'S GONNA PUT YOUR BOSS, THE PENGUIN, AWAY FOR A LONG TIME!
HARVEY, HAVE YOU ACTUALLY SEEN THESE? SURE, THEY'RE RACY...
...BUT MAYOR COBBLEPOT ISN'T MARRIED. SO, THEY'RE HARDLY SCANDALOUS.
AW CRUD.
HEH. KNOWING THE MAYOR, HE'D PROBABLY WANT A SET FOR HIMSELF!
MEN, PAY ATTENTION! WE STILL HAVE TO DEAL WITH...
BATMAN?! ¡AY! HE DID IT AGAIN!
"SLIPPED RIGHT THROUGH OUR FINGERS!"
FINAL BOARDING FOR STAR CITY AND ALL POINTS WEST.
JULIE MADISON.

BRUCE?
YOU CAME! I KNEW--

A MAN IS DEAD TONIGHT BECAUSE SOME-ONE ORDERED A HIT--
--ON A MAN WHO TOOK SOME PHOTOS, AND ANYONE WHO SAW THEM.

PICTURES OF YOU AND THE PENGUIN.
EXPLAIN YOURSELF.

M-MY BOYFRIEND. HE CAN'T STAND COBBLEPOT. HE'S OBSESSED WITH HIM!
IF HE EVER FOUND OUT THAT I USED TO... BE WITH HIM...

IT WOULD HAVE RUINED EVERYTHING! PLEASE! YOU DON'T UNDERSTAND!

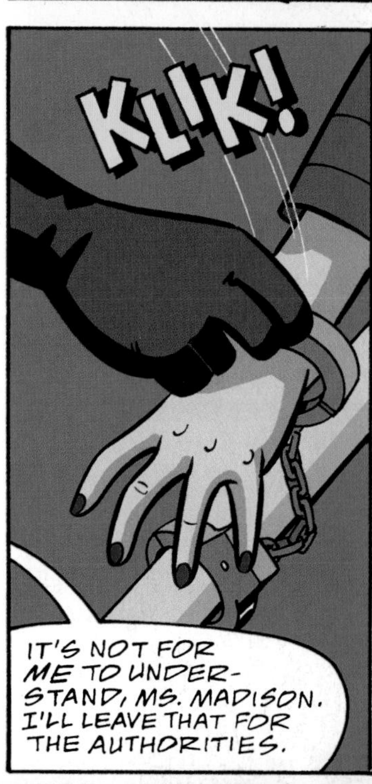
KLIK!
IT'S NOT FOR ME TO UNDER-STAND, MS. MADISON. I'LL LEAVE THAT FOR THE AUTHORITIES.

BUT HE WAS GOING TO PROPOSE TO ME, TONIGHT!
I WAS GOING TO LAND A BILLIONAIRE!
THIS CAN'T BE HAPPENING!
THIS WAS MY SHOT! DON'T YOU GET THAT?! MY ONE SHOT!

THE STACKED DECK
I BEEN HEARIN' THINGS ABOUT YOU, O'BRIAN.
THAT YOU'RE IN GOOD WITH BLACK MASK.
...SINCE ONE A' HIS GUYS GOT PINCHED, HE'S GONNA NEED SOME NEW BLOOD.

AND YOU'D LIKE ME TO PUT IN A GOOD WORD FOR YOU?
TELL 'IM MY PAL, MATCHES MALONE, IS A STAND-UP GUY?
IT'LL COST YA.
UNNER-STOOD.
ONE MORE THING. IF YOU GET IN, THEY'RE GONNA MAKE YOU WEAR SOME WEIRD MASK.
YOU AIN'T GOT A PROBLEM WITH THAT?
NOPE. NOT AT ALL.

TONIGHT'S FIRST ORDER OF BUSINESS: BATMAN.
I KNEW THERE'D COME A TIME WHEN THE DARK KNIGHT WOULD TAKE AN INTEREST IN OUR ORGANIZATION.
THAT TIME WAS LAST NIGHT. AND IT'S COST US OUR HEAD OF ELIMINATIONS.
FORTUNATELY, I HAVE ALREADY FOUND A SUITABLE REPLACEMENT.
GENTLEMEN, I'D LIKE TO INTRODUCE YOU TO...

...MY PERSONAL ANGEL OF DEATH--
PHANTASM!
NEXT:
PLAYING WITH MATCHES!

LIAR LIAR
TY TEMPLETON--WRITER
RICK BURCHETT--PENCILLER
TERRY BEATTY--INKER
ZYLONOL--COLORIST
PHIL FELIX--LETTERER
JOAN HILTY--EDITOR
NO VIGILA
THE VREELAND AUDITORIUM. ONE YEAR AGO.
ONE MONTH AFTER OSWALD COBBLEPOT ANNOUNCED HIS CANDIDACY FOR MAYOR OF GOTHAM CITY.
COBBLEPOT CARES
THERE MIGHT BE LATE-COMERS...
NAH, I THINK THIS IS YER BIG PEP RALLY FOR TONIGHT.
NO CONCERN, OFFICER BULLFINCH... IT'S STILL EARLY IN THE POLITICAL SEASON. ALL I NEED IS A FEW HEAD-LINES AND MY CAM-PAIGN WILL TAKE WING--
THAT'S DETECTIVE BULLOCK TO YOU, MR. CHAMBER-POT...

TOUCHÉ, DETECTIVE. BUT A MORE RESPECTFUL TONE NEXT TIME YOU ADDRESS ME, PLEASE...
I'M GONNA RESPECT YA FROM BACK HERE ...THOSE THINGS'LL KILL YA.

THAT'S NEVER GOING TO HAPPEN. NOT WITH MY HERCULEAN CONSTITUTION.
STICK CLOSE... GORDON ASSIGNED YOU TO PROTECT ME FROM A FAR MORE DANGER-OUS ENEMY.
YEAH... I READ YER COM-PLAINT...

BATMAN HAS SENT ME DEATH THREATS...
HE KNOWS HIS DAYS IN GOTHAM ARE NUMBERED--AND HE'S AFTER ME!
LADIES AND GENTLEMEN... THE NEXT MAYOR OF GOTHAM CITY...

VIGILANTES
...OSWALD COBBLEPOT!
GOOD EVENING, CONCERNED CITIZENS...
OUR GREAT CITY TODAY... FACES A GRAVE TOMORROW.

IT IS OVER-RUN BY ANARCHISTS AND VILLAINS.
MEN AND WOMEN WITH NO MORALS, AND NO CONCERN FOR THE WELL-BEING OF THE GOOD PEOPLE OF GOTHAM CITY...

AND CHIEF AMONGST THEM...
...IS THE VILE VIGILANTE KNOWN AS BAT-MAN!

BOOOOO!
BATMAN SAVED ME FROM A MUGGING LAST YEAR...
SHUT UP! LET HIM TALK!
TUK TUK
HE'S GOT A POINT!

YES, YES... I UNDER-STAND THE CAPED CROOK GETS VERY GOOD PRESS.
BUT YOU CAN'T BELIEVE WHAT YOU READ IN THE PAPERS, GOOD PEOPLE!

SURE, BATMAN HELPS OLD LADIES CROSS THE STREET AND RESCUES CHILDREN FROM WELLS...
BUT IT'S ALL A CON GAME!
HE HAS AN AGENDA!
SSSSS!

HE WANTS YOU TO TRUST HIM... SO YOU DON'T WONDER WHY HE WEARS A MASK.
DON'T YOU FIND THAT ODD?

HOLY COW! HE'S ON FIRE!
NAH, YOU SHOULD HEAR HIM WHEN HE REALLY GETS GOING...

SOON, HE SHOUTS, "THERE'S NO DIFFERENCE BETWEEN THE JOKER AND BATMAN!"
IT'S THE SAME SPEECH EVERY NIGHT...

I HAVE EVIDENCE OF THREATS--
PENGUIN! YER LEG!!
WHAT?!

RRRIP!
HOW DARE YOU REFER TO ME BY THAT--?

YE GODS!!

WAAAUGGGH!
KA THONK!

SLAP!
SLAP!
SLAP!
SLAP!

RRRRRR...
FLASH!

YOU DID THAT DELIBERATELY!
NO KIDDIN'. YER WELCOME.

YOU COULD HAVE USED THE WATER ON THE PODIUM, YOU IDIOT! I WANT YOU OUT OF MY SIGHT!

YOU'RE ON MY LIST, APE! WHEN I'M MAYOR... I WILL HAVE YOUR BADGE!
OH, LIKE I'M ALL WORRIED...

...THAT'S NEVER GONNA HAPPEN. NOT WITH YOUR TEENY TINY POLL NUMBERS...
HAH!

ONE YEAR LATER.
SIGH...
MAYOR COBBLEPOT SAYS: "KEEP AN EAGLE EYE OUT FOR LITTER. KEEP GOTHAM CLEAN!"
BATMAN RESCUES MAYORAL CANDIDATE
BULLOCK INVESTIGATIONS
THE END

CREATORS

DAN SLOTT WRITER

Dan Slott is a comics writer best known for his work on DC Comics' Arkham Asylum, and, for Marvel, The Avengers and the Amazing Spider-Man.

TY TEMPLETON PENCILLER

Ty Templeton was born in the wilds of downtown Toronto, Canada to a show-business family. He makes his living writing and drawing comic books, working on such characters as Batman, Superman, Spider-Man, The Simpsons, the Avengers, and many others.

TERRY BEATTY INKER

For more than ten years, Terry Beatty was the main inker of DC Comics' "animated-style" Batman comics, including The Batman Strikes. More recently, he worked on *Return to Perdition*, a graphic novel for DC's Vertigo Crime.

LEE LOUGHRIDGE COLORIST

Lee Loughridge has been working in comics for more than fifteen years. He currently lives in sunny California in a tent on the beach.

GLOSSARY

amends (uh-MENDS)--when you make amends, you do something to make up for a wrong or a mistake

anarchist (AN-er-kisst)--a person who seeks to overturn by violence all forms of society and government

constitution (kon-stuh-TOO-shuhn)--general health and strength; physical well-being

deliberately (duh-LIB-ur-uht-lee)--if you do something deliberately, you planned to do it or did it on purpose

glamorous (GLAM-ur-uhss)--attractive and exciting

homing (HOH-ming)--guiding or directing to a specific destination

mourn (MORN)--to be very sad and grieve for someone who has died

petty (PET-ee)--trivial and unimportant, or mean and spiteful

putrid (PYOO-trid)--rotten or evil

valise (vuhl-EES)--a small piece of luggage that can be carried by hand

vendetta (ven-DET-uh)--a long-lasting feud between two or more parties

vigilante (vij-uh-LAN-tee)--any person who takes the law into their own hands

BATMAN GLOSSARY

Alfred Pennyworth: Bruce Wayne's loyal butler. He knows Bruce Wayne's secret identity and helps the Dark Knight solve crimes in Gotham City.

Batarang: a metal, bat-shaped weapon that can be thrown like a boomerang.

Black Mask: also known as Roman Sionis, Black Mask is a ruthless businessman and criminal boss of the Gotham underworld.

Deadshot: a hired assassin and the self-proclaimed world's greatest marksman, Deadshot relishes the role of the anti-hero.

Harvey Bullock: a controversial policeman, Officer Bullock cares little for the letter of the law as long as the job gets done.

Matches Malone: a two-bit gangster Batman poses as to infiltrate criminal organizations.

Oswald Cobblepot: the mayor of Gotham City, but known to Batman as the Penguin, a mastermind of the city's criminal underworld.

Phantasm: despite posing as a man, Phantasm is actually Andrea Beaumont, a deadly martial artist who wields a scythe with expert skill.

VISUAL QUESTIONS & PROMPTS

1. Why was Oswald Cobblepot upset that Harvey Bullock saved him?

2. Who is the "client" Black Mask is talking about in this first panel? What clues in the previous pages lead you to believe that this is the case?

3. Why did Batman leave this crook right after catching him (on page 7)? What information in the following pages led you to that conclusion?

4. What was Alfred trying to warn Bruce about in this panel (on page 9)? Did Alfred end up being right? Why or why not?

5. How do we know the man in the second panel is Bruce Wayne? Why is he posing as Matches Malone?

BATMAN ADVENTURES

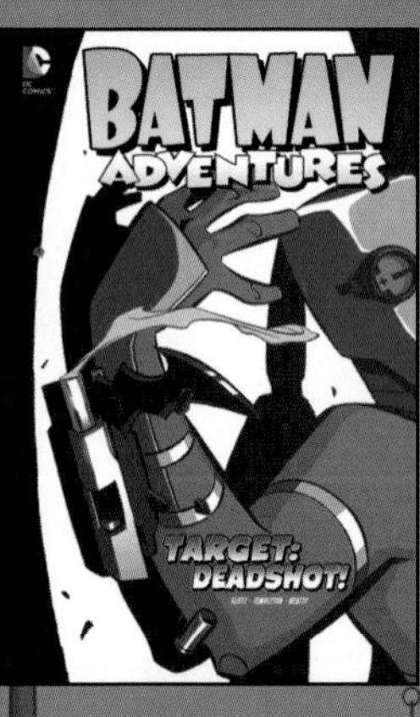